DRONES

Personal Drones

BY CECILIA PINTO MCCARTHY

CONTENT CONSULTANT
MICHAEL BRAASCH, PHD, PE
THOMAS PROFESSOR OF ELECTRICAL ENGINEERING
OHIO UNIVERSITY

Kids Core
An Imprint of Abdo Publishing
abdobooks.com

abdobooks.com

Published by Abdo Publishing, a division of ABDO, PO Box 398166, Minneapolis, Minnesota 55439. Copyright © 2021 by Abdo Consulting Group, Inc. International copyrights reserved in all countries. No part of this book may be reproduced in any form without written permission from the publisher. Kids Core™ is a trademark and logo of Abdo Publishing.

Printed in the United States of America, North Mankato, Minnesota
082020
012021

THIS BOOK CONTAINS
RECYCLED MATERIALS

Cover Photo: Shutterstock Images
Interior Photos: Richard Drew/AP Images, 4–5; Yanosh Nemesh/Shutterstock Images, 6; GNT Studio/Shutterstock Images, 8; Shutterstock Images, 9, 21, 29 (top); Valentin Valkov/Shutterstock Images, 10; Joerg Mitter/Red Bull/AP Images, 12–13; Arnd Wiegmann/Reuters/Newscom, 14; Ilmars Znotins/AFP/Getty Images, 16; Alex JW Robinson/Shutterstock Images, 18–19; Alexey Fedorenko/Shutterstock Images, 20; Dean Murray/SwellProUSA/Cover Images/Newscom, 22; Launette Florian/PhotoPQR/La Provence/MAXPPP/Newscom, 23, 29 (bottom); Caro Images/Oberhaeuser/Newscom, 24; Rodrigo Reyes Marin/AFLO/Newscom, 26, 28; Easton Green/The Minnesota Daily/AP Images, 27

Editor: Maddie Spalding
Series Designer: Katharine Hale

Library of Congress Control Number: 2019954185

Publisher's Cataloging-in-Publication Data

Names: McCarthy, Cecilia Pinto, author
Title: Personal drones / by Cecilia Pinto McCarthy
Description: Minneapolis, Minnesota : Abdo Publishing, 2021 | Series: Drones | Includes online resources and index.
Identifiers: ISBN 9781532192807 (lib. bdg.) | ISBN 9781644944400 (pbk.) | ISBN 9781098210700 (ebook)
Subjects: LCSH: Drone aircraft--Juvenile literature. | Hobbies--Juvenile literature. | Toy aircraft--Juvenile literature. | Vehicles, Remotely piloted --Juvenile literature. | Airplanes--Radio control--Juvenile literature.
Classification: DDC 629.13339--dc23

CONTENTS

Some racing drones are small, while others are large. Drones of the same size race against each other.

CHAPTER 1

Fast Fun

Buzz, whir! Four drones fly by. They are racing around a winding track. They zip through tight tunnels and over **obstacles**. The drone pilots sit nearby. They wear special goggles. Each set of goggles connects to a camera on the front of a drone.

Some drone races are held outdoors. Drone races happen all around the world.

The cameras stream live video. Racers get a first-person view as their drones zoom along the track. The racers use handheld controllers. They steer their drones by moving the joysticks.

These levers control the drones. After three quick laps, the red drone wins the race.

What Are Drones?

A drone is a type of robot. People operate drones from a distance. They use controllers to communicate with the drones. People can also control drones with smartphones or tablets.

Drone Rules

People who fly personal drones must follow rules. The Federal Aviation Administration makes these rules. Drones must fly at or below 400 feet (122 m). Pilots must keep drones within sight. They cannot fly drones over groups of people. It is also illegal to fly drones near other aircraft or close to airports.

Personal drones come in many shapes and sizes.

Personal drones are drones that people own themselves. They use these drones for fun. Racing is just one way to have fun with drones. Many people also enjoy taking photographs and videos with their drones.

Personal drones can be big or small. Many beginner drones cost less than $200. More advanced drones can cost thousands of dollars. They have special equipment such as high-quality cameras.

Some drones, such as the ANAFI drone, cost more than $500. They have better equipment than beginner drones.

The Parts of a Quadcopter

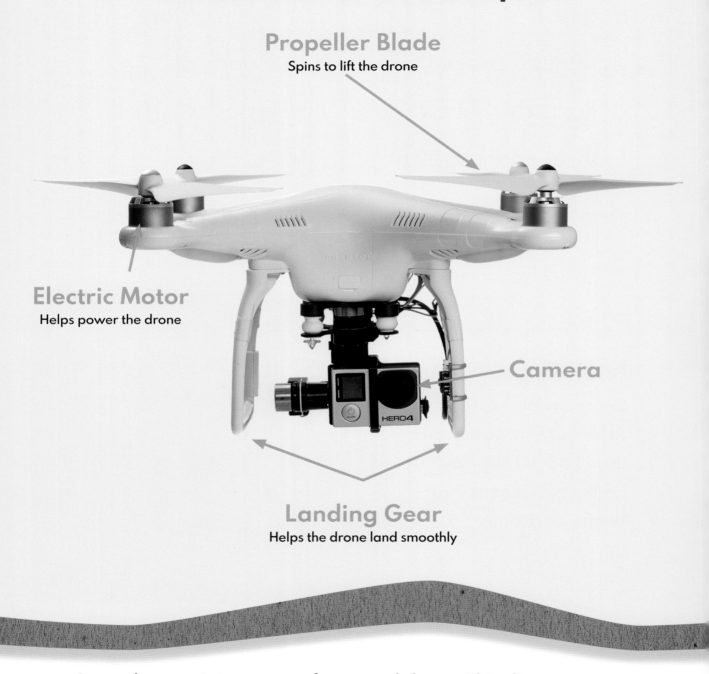

Propeller Blade
Spins to lift the drone

Electric Motor
Helps power the drone

Camera

Landing Gear
Helps the drone land smoothly

A quadcopter is one type of personal drone. This diagram shows the basic parts of a quadcopter drone.

Types of Personal Drones

Most personal drones are **aerial** drones. They use propellers to fly. Propellers are parts with spinning blades. Quadcopters are popular aerial drones. They have four propellers. The propeller blades push air down to lift the drone.

Some personal drones work underwater. Their propellers move the drones through the water. Divers use these drones to film their adventures.

Further Evidence

Look at the website below. Does it give any new evidence to support the information in Chapter One?

MultiGP

abdocorelibrary.com/personal-drones

In a 2017 drone race in Austria, drones had to avoid many obstacles, including fire.

CHAPTER 2

Drone Sports

Some people compete in sports with personal drones. There are many types of drone sports, including drone racing. The Drone Racing League is an international organization for professional drone racing.

Drones can also be used to film competitions such as skiing races.

In a race, each drone must complete a set number of laps around a track. Racing drones can reach speeds of up to 120 miles per hour (190 km/h). The fastest drone is the winner. Some races are aired on television sports networks such as NBC Sports and ESPN.

Drone Duels

Another type of drone sport involves **combat**. In 2012, the Aerial Sports League held its first flying drone combat games. The pilots try to knock each other's drones out of the air. The last drone flying is the winner.

Pilots come up with clever ways to stop their **opponents**. Some drones launch nets. The nets entangle other drones' propeller blades.

Drones at Work

Personal drones can be used for work. Wildlife scientists track animals with drones. They watch where and how animals move. Drones can help deliver medicine. They can fly to areas that are difficult to reach by land. Police also use drones. Drones help them survey areas and prevent crime.

In the 2017 test, the giant drone pulled the snowboarders across an icy lake in Latvia.

Snowboarding

Some people have come up with new ways to use drones for sports. In 2017, **engineers** built a giant drone. It had 16 propellers. They used the drone to pull four snowboarders. One person controlled the drone. The drone pulled the snowboarders at 37 miles per hour (60 km/h).

Marque Cornblatt is the head of the Aerial Sports League. He explains what happens when racing drones crash:

> The pilot has 90 seconds to run out there, fix the damage, and get it back in the air.

Source: Kelsey D. Atherton. "Meet Drone Dueling, the Sport California Is About to Inadvertently Kill." *Popular Science*, 28 June 2017, popsci.com. Accessed 7 Oct. 2019.

Comparing Texts

Think about the quote. Does it support the information in this chapter? Or does it give a different perspective? Explain how in a few sentences.

Many people use drones to take high-quality pictures of landscapes.

CHAPTER 3

Drone Features

Personal drones can take great photos and videos. Their cameras capture a bird's-eye view. In the past, people needed to hire a helicopter to film from the air. Now these difficult shots are easy to take with a drone.

Some people use drones to take selfies.

Anyone can fly a drone overhead to record spectacular views.

Buyers can choose drones with special camera lenses. A zoom lens lets users take close-up shots. Wide-angle lenses can focus on large areas. They are great for landscape photos and videos.

Drone company DJI makes many popular personal drones. One such drone is the Mavic Mini. It weighs just 8.8 ounces (0.2 kg). It can fit in a person's hand. It has four propellers. The Mavic Mini's arms fold up. This makes it easy to carry in a pocket or small bag.

The Mavic Mini can fly for up to 30 minutes before its battery needs to be recharged.

Under the Sea

Some people want to film underwater. The iBubble is a popular underwater drone. Divers do not have to carry heavy video equipment when they use an iBubble.

The iBubble is the first wireless underwater camera drone. Seven propellers move it

Some drones, such as the Spry drone, are waterproof. They can film in the air and underwater.

The iBubble sends out sound waves that hit objects and bounce back. This helps the drone find and avoid objects.

through the water. A diver controls the drone with a remote. The iBubble can follow a diver and film from behind. Or it can move ahead of the diver and film as the diver swims forward.

Some drones can carry heavy loads. They can deliver packages to people.

New Technology

Experts are researching ways to make drones smarter. They are developing more drones that use artificial intelligence (AI). People do many tasks that require a lot of thought. Drones with AI can do some of these tasks. They can learn and solve problems.

Drones with AI are also **autonomous**. This means they can fly by themselves. They take in information about their environment. Then they react.

AI drones have **sensors**. The sensors identify objects in their paths. Then the drones move to avoid the objects.

AI versus Piloted Drones

In 2019, the first AlphaPilot Innovation Challenge was held. It is a drone engineering contest. Teams design racing drones that use AI. The drones must be able to fly by themselves. The drones race against other drones that are controlled by pilots. The piloted drones beat the AI drones in the 2019 race.

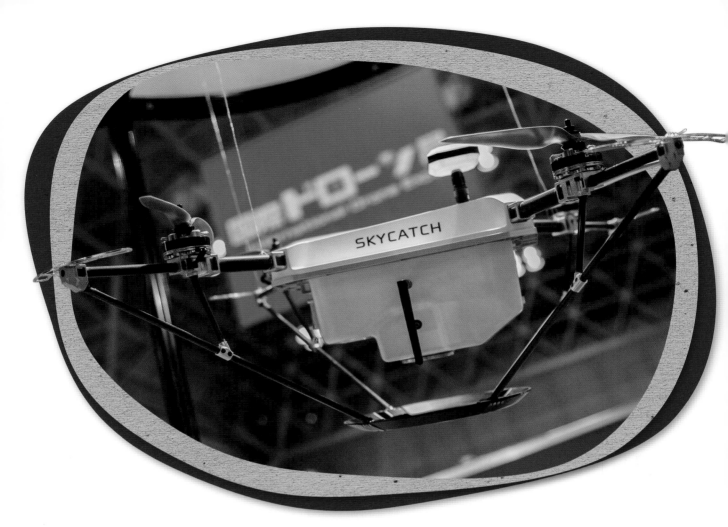

Pilots can use a phone app to fly Skycatch drones.

Other drones have more advanced features. The company Skycatch creates software for drones. Skycatch drones can survey land. They can create three-dimensional images.

At the University of Minnesota, researchers are working on AI drones. These drones can map their surroundings.

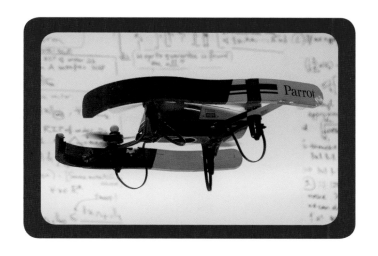

Drone technology keeps improving. Drones are becoming less expensive. More people are using drones for fun. Personal drones are sure to change the way people play and work in the future.

Explore Online

Visit the website below. Did you learn any new information about uses for personal drones that wasn't in Chapter Three?

Lifesaving Drones

abdocorelibrary.com/personal-drones

Drone Stats

Skycatch Drone

- Used to survey land
- Can create three-dimensional images

Mavic Mini

- Used to take high-quality photos and videos
- Its arms fold up, making it easy to carry

iBubble

- Films underwater
- Can follow divers and capture underwater footage

Glossary

aerial
describing something that happens in the air

autonomous
able to operate without a person controlling it

combat
a fight

engineers
skilled workers who design and build things

obstacles
things that get in the way or block a path

opponents
people who compete against others in a contest, game, or fight

sensors
equipment that can detect things such as heat, light, sound, and pressure

Online Resources

To learn more about personal drones, visit our free resource websites below.

Visit **abdocorelibrary.com** or scan this QR code for free Common Core resources for teachers and students, including vetted activities, multimedia, and booklinks, for deeper subject comprehension.

Visit **abdobooklinks.com** or scan this QR code for free additional online weblinks for further learning. These links are routinely monitored and updated to provide the most current information available.

Learn More

Abell, Tracy, and Alexis Roumanis. *Drones*. AV2 by Weigl, 2019.

London, Martha. *Deep-Sea Drones*. Abdo Publishing, 2021.

Olson, Elsie. *Drones*. Abdo Publishing, 2018.

Index

About the Author

Cecilia Pinto McCarthy has written more than 30 books for young readers. She and her family live north of Boston, Massachusetts.